To Lucas, Monique,
Cléa, Nicolas, Louis, Tom,
Christine, Natascha Morris,
& librarians everywhere

—VE

To Mum and Dad who always
supported us in exploring our
interests. And to my younger
brother Dylan . . . who stole my
pocket dinosaur encyclopedia
and never gave it back

—NM

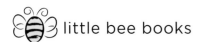 little bee books

New York, NY
Text copyright © 2022 by Viviane Elbee
Illustrations copyright © 2022 by Nicole Miles
Manufactured in China RRD 1121
First Edition
10 9 8 7 6 5 4 3 2 1
Library of Congress Cataloging-in-Publication Data is available upon request.
ISBN 978-1-4998-1174-2
littlebeebooks.com   JUN - '22
For information about special discounts on bulk purchases,
please contact Little Bee Books at sales@littlebeebooks.com.

I want my Book Back

by Viviane Elbee • illustrated by Nicole Miles

WITHDRAWN

DINOSAURS
BY DR D. NOSOR

STOMP!

little bee books

Daryl loved only *one* book.
It took him on roaring, stomping
dinosaur adventures.

He glided like a *microraptor*
and charged like a *triceratops*.

It was so fun to read and play with.

But Daryl's book was

NOT FOR SHARING!

Daryl renewed his book from the library
again and again, until one day:
CANNOT RENEW—BOOK ON HOLD

"Time to share with other kids,"
Mommy said, dropping the book
in the return bin.

"ROAR!!!" Daryl tried his best *T. rex* moves to retrieve it. "I want MY BOOK back!"

Back home, Mommy tried
to cheer up Daryl.

Daryl needed his book back **NOW.**

With a long, *brontosaurus* neck, maybe Daryl could stretch across the street and snag his book!

But his neck was not long enough.

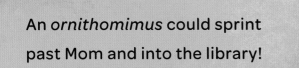

An *ornithomimus* could sprint
past Mom and into the library!

But it was dinnertime.

"I want my book back!" Daryl said, prying the ketchup open with his *T. rex* claw.

And just like that, he plotted the perfect plan.

The next morning, Daryl grabbed his claws and raced to the library.

Success!
The book return bin
swung open.

But . . . it was empty.

Daryl ran inside.

He scanned the shelves . . .

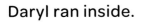

checked the top of
the bookcases . . .

inspected the cart . . . .

ZILCH.

Daryl ran to the librarian.

She was starting story time, and she was holding . . .

his book!

"Daryl!" Mommy called out.

The librarian smiled at Daryl.

"Would you like to stand up front with me and share this book with our friends?"

The librarian opened the book.

STAND UP, STOMP, AND ROAR! DINOSAURS EXPLORE!

DINOSAURS

Daryl stomped.

STOMP!

Daryl ROARED.

rrrrrrrrrrROAR!!

And then . . . the other kids STOMPED and ROARED!

Daryl showed them how to swing their *brontosaurus* necks,
glide like *microraptors*, and snap their *T. rex* jaws.
Soon, everyone had turned into dinosaurs—even Mommy!

"Great job, Daryl," the librarian said. "Do you want to come back tomorrow and share this book at story time?"

"Yes!" Daryl said, hugging his book tightly.

Back home, Daryl noticed it was *not* his dinosaur book.

This new book took him on flying, fire-breathing adventures!
It helped him soar above volcanoes and dive through the clouds.

It was so fun to read and play with
that he knew it would be . . .

PERFECT FOR SHARING!